20 HUNGRY PIGGIES

Trudy Harris

illustrated by Andrew N. Harris

M Millbrook Press/Minneapolis

To my grandchildren and to my students. Thanks for all you teach me!

—TH

For my little piggies: William and Isabelle. And to mom and my beautiful wife Marie, thank you for all of your love and support.

—ANH

Text copyright © 2007 by Trudy Harris
Illustrations copyright © 2007 by Andrew N. Harris

Millbrook Press, Inc.
A division of Lerner Publishing Group
241 First Avenue North
Minneapolis, Minnesota 55401 U.S.A.

Website address: www.lernerbooks.com

Library of Congress Cataloging-in-Publication Data

Harris, Trudy.
   20 hungry piggies : a number book / by Trudy Harris ; illustrated by Andrew N. Harris.
      p.   cm.
   Summary: The wolf from "The Three Little Pigs" shows up at a party attended by lots of piggies, but his plans for dinner are disrupted by the pigs from "This Little Piggy Went to Market."
ISBN-13: 978-0-8225-6370-9 (lib. bdg. : alk. paper)
ISBN-10: 0-8225-6370-3 (lib. bdg. : alk. paper)
   [1. Characters in literature—Fiction. 2. Nursery rhymes—Fiction. 3. Pigs—Fiction. 4. Wolves—Fiction. 5. Counting. 6. Stories in rhyme.] I. Harris, Andrew, 1977-   , ill. II. Title. III. Title: Twenty hungry piggies.
PZ8.3.H24318Tw 2007
[E]—dc22   2006018399

Manufactured in the United States of America
1 2 3 4 5 6 – DP – 12 11 10 09 08 07

First little piggy went to market.

Second little piggy stayed home.

Sixth little piggy liked to skydive.

Seventh little piggy flew the plane.

Eighth and ninth piggies whispered,
"We're glad we took the train."

Tenth little piggy furnished donuts.
Eleventh piggy juggled tangerines.

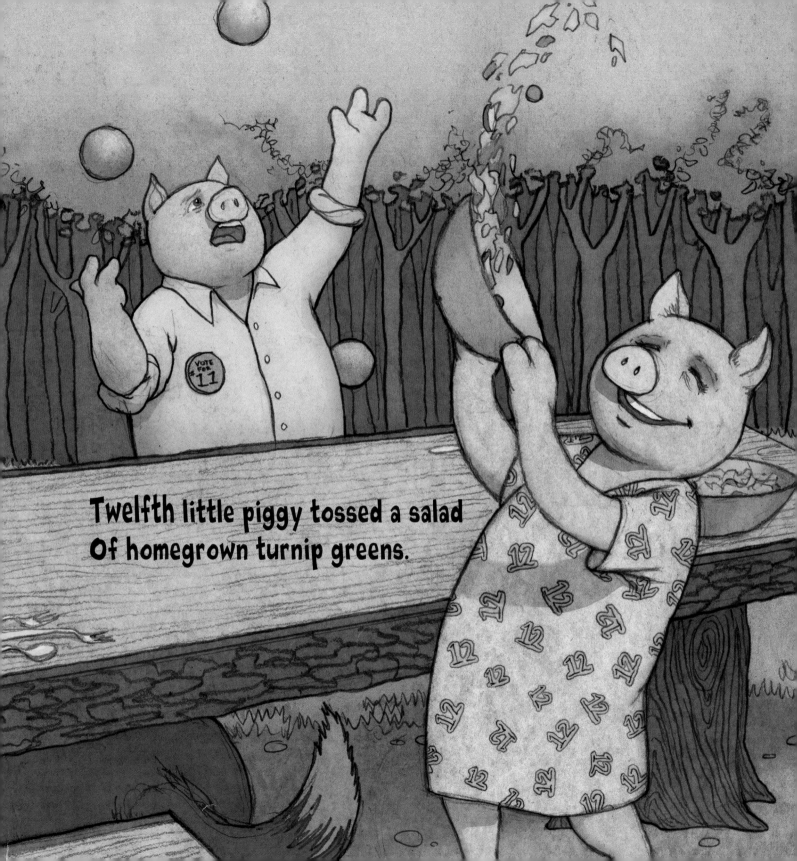

Twelfth little piggy tossed a salad
Of homegrown turnip greens.

Thirteenth piggy strummed the banjo.
Fourteenth piggy played the drums.

Fifteenth piggy picked a centerpiece
Of fresh chrysanthemums.

Sixteenth piggy brought a bucket
Of smelly sauerkraut.

Seventeenth piggy saw a toothy grin,
Long whiskers, and a snout.

"Aaaaaaooooooo!"
Howled a wolf from the bushes,
Then said with a wicked sneer,
"I want pork chops for
MY picnic!
And I'm going to
get them
HERE!

So GET in a line,
You tasty swine,
'Cause I'm **bigger** than you
And I'm ready to dine!"

Eighteenth piggy, in a panic,
Yelled, "Run everybody. Let's Go!"
But nineteenth piggy told the others,
"It's hopeless. We're too slow."

So . . .
1st, 2nd, 3rd, 4th, 5th, 6th, 7th, 8th, 9th, 10th, 11th, 12th, 13th, 14th, 15th, 16th, 17th, 18th, 19th . . . ?

Twentieth piggy, from her hammock,
Woke up in the mood for lunch.

All the piggies heard the bell ring.
"FOOD!" they yelled.

Then the big bad wolf got
trampled

By nineteen piggies' feet.

Last little piggy reached the table.
They had fun and food galore.

Wolf never got his pork chops—
Nor bothered piggies anymore.